Brielle-Elaine Tries to Fit In!

Written by

La-Toya S. Facey

Illustrations by Floyd Yamyamin

AuthorHouse™
1663 Liberty Drive
Bloomington, IN 47403
www.authorhouse.com
Phone: 833-262-8899

This book is printed on acid-free paper.

ISBN: 978-1-4634-2353-7 (sc)
ISBN: 978-1-4817-4503-1 (e)

Library of Congress Control Number: 2011911254

Print information available on the last page.

Published by AuthorHouse 05/23/2023

author HOUSE®

For EskaWillory, my loving grandmother

&

For my mom, without you there is no me

BING! "Cupcakes are ready!" shouted Mom excitedly. Brielle-Elaine peered over the counter to watch her mom pull out the freshly baked extra-chocolate, chocolate chip, double fudge cupcakes out of the oven. She just knew that after giving her new classmates these cupcakes, they would definitely want her to be their friend. Brielle-Elaine waited until the cupcakes cooled to taste them.

"Perfect, Mom, no one will be able to resist them. I will start tomorrow as a new student and leave as the most popular, all because of these cupcakes. DELICIOUS!!!!" Mom smiled.

Tomorrow would be the big day! Tomorrow would be the day that Brielle-Elaine started her new school. She would be in Mrs. Willory's fourth-grade class at Anaberry Elementary School. The school year had already begun, but her dad had a new job and she had to switch to a new school in the middle of the year. She missed her friends terribly, but she knew that she would make friends easily, especially with her world famous cupcakes.

Brielle-Elaine got up and put on her outfit for the first day of her new school. It was pretty and pink and made her feel like a princess. She even added glitter to make sure that her skin shimmered just as much as her outfit. She looked in the mirror, and she was satisfied with what she saw. Her mom added the icing to the cupcakes while she slept, and they looked amazing. She couldn't wait to pass them out to the class.

"Good morning, class. Today we have a new student. Her name is Brielle-Elaine," announced Mrs. Willory.

Brielle-Elaine smiled and surveyed the room at the same time to see who would be her friend first. She cleared her throat and said, "Excuse me, Mrs. Willory, I brought in cupcakes for the class. Is it okay if I pass them out now?"

"Normally we wouldn't do it now, but it is a special day. It is not everyday that we get a new student, and besides, those cupcakes look scrumptious!" Mrs. Willory exclaimed with a grin on her face.

As soon as she turned around to begin passing out the cupcakes, she tripped over her pretty, pink, shimmery, untied laces. The cupcakes flew out of her hands. They landed everywhere, even on her pretty, pink, princess-like outfit purposely worn for the first day of her new school. The class burst into laughter, and Brielle-Elaine burst into tears. She was so embarrassed. Her teacher sent her to the office to call her mom. She couldn't reach her, so they gave her a change of clothes that were two sizes too big. Her first day was not going well, and to make matters worse, no one even asked her to be their friend.

At recess and lunchtime, she sat by herself and watched the other kids play. They were all in groups. She saw the kids who liked sports, wore jerseys, and talked about which team won what game. Then she saw the really smart students who spent their lunch and recess working on extra-credit math problems. Then she saw the kids who didn't take school as seriously as they should. They goofed around and made silly faces when the teacher wasn't looking. Tomorrow she would make friends even if she had to be someone that she wasn't to fit in.

The dismissal bell rang, and Brielle-Elaine couldn't be happier. She raced to her mom's car and slammed the door. Her mom immediately asked her what happened. After explaining to her mom what happened, she burst into tears and yelled, "AND I STILL DON'T HAVE ANY FRIENDS!!!!"

"Don't worry, baby, just be yourself. Everyone will like you. You'll see," Mom suggested sympathetically.

That night Brielle-Elaine tossed and turned in bed. She dreamed about her master plan. She knew what she had to do to make friends. In the morning she got up early to put her plan into effect. She snuck into her brother's bedroom and borrowed his sneakers, his baseball cap, and his jersey. She got dressed and waited for her mom to take her to school. She was too nervous to eat. She was just ready to start her new day. Her mom looked at her outfit and asked, "Why are you wearing Elijah's clothes?"

"Oh, Mom, I just borrowed them because—because—ummm no reason." She was happy that they were running late, because her mom didn't press the issue.

Brielle-Elaine arrived at school and walked to Mrs. Willory's class. She sat in her seat and did her assignments for the day. She couldn't wait until recess. Only then would she know if her plan would work and if she would make friends. Finally, it was lunchtime and time to put her plan into action.

Brielle-Elaine walked over to the jocks. She turned her hat backward and stuck her ponytail under her cap. "Hey, guys," she stated nervously.

"Hey, it's Brielle-Elaine, right?" asked Kazmin, one of the jocks. She was happy that he knew her name. She thought her plan was actually going to work. The jocks immediately started talking about sports. She tried to keep up, but she couldn't. She didn't know a play from a dunk or a guard from a linebacker. This was too confusing. When she stopped thinking so hard she realized that they had asked her a question. "Ahhhh, what did you say?" she asked nervously.

"Man, let's get out of here! She doesn't know anything about sports," snarled Nicholas. The jocks walked away, leaving Brielle-Elaine standing all alone. Once again, her plan had failed.

Brielle-Elaine was discouraged for a moment, but she knew what she would have to do tomorrow. The night came and went. Before she knew it, it was morning and it was time for school again. This time all she needed was her mom's green reading glasses to complete her look. Today she was going to look supersmart. She tried to dress similarly to how the smart kids had dressed. She wore her stockings, tucked in her button-down blue and white shirt neatly into her skirt, and put on her mom's green reading glasses. She looked just like the smart kids. She put her mom's reading glasses in her backpack so that her mom didn't know that she had snuck them out of the house. Now it was time to put her new plan into action.

At lunchtime, Brielle-Elaine went to sit next to the smart kids. They had their heads down, and they all seemed to be working on a difficult math problem that took up a whole page! Brielle-Elaine reluctantly sat down and hoped that today would be better than yesterday. "Can I help?" she unwillingly asked. "Sure," said Ray Anthony. He replied without lifting his head. He slid her a sheet of paper with a math problem as long as the yacht she saw sailing last summer. She didn't let the thought stop her. Brielle-Elaine took the paper and started working. She erased and wrote, erased, and wrote some more. "FINISHED!!!!"she yelled.

All the smart kids stopped and looked up from their papers. They were amazed. "It took me five days to complete that problem," Dexter said in awe.

"She couldn't have. Let me see what you did," requested Oliver.

Brielle-Elaine proudly handed her paper over, knowing that her plan finally worked. She was excited and started to daydream about all her friends that she was going to have in school. She probably wouldn't be the most popular, but she would settle for the smartest. She soon realized that all the smart kids were laughing.

"She subtracted when she should have multiplied," Seattle said and giggled.

"She also divided when she should have added," Madison responded with a chuckle.

"She knows nothing about math!" yelled Cecelia with a scowl.

"What's so funny? STOP LAUGHING AT ME!!!!" Brielle-Elaine screamed.

She ran into the restroom and hid in one of the stalls. She was so upset, but when she thought about it, she knew this whole mess was her fault. She had a backup plan. She was supposed to join the kids who goofed off in school. After the last two disastrous days, she decided against it. Besides, if the teacher called her mom, her only problem wouldn't be that she didn't have any friends. She decided right then and there in the bathroom stall that tomorrow, she would be herself.

The next day, Brielle-Elaine got dressed in her regular school clothes, jeans and a T-shirt—pink, of course! She ate breakfast with her family, and she was excited to go to class. She arrived at school a little before the bell rang. She saw some of her classmates just hanging around. Brielle-Elaine was nervous, but she knew today would be the best day of all. The school bell rang, and class began.

Brielle-Elaine was paying attention during the lesson, and she was able to answer all of Mrs. Willory's questions correctly. She fed the class pet, which happened to be an iguana. As she fed him, she noticed all the other kids gawking at her. They couldn't believe that she wasn't scared of feeding the iguana. She was chosen to read the story of the week aloud to the class during story time, and best of all she got to erase the board before lunch. She never did any of these things before, because she was so caught up in pretending to be someone else.

At lunchtime she started to eat her food at the lunch table by herself, and then one of the smart kids came over and sat down with her. Then one of the jocks joined them. Before long, Brielle-Elaine's table was full. Most of the math kids were telling her that she read well. The jocks told her that not even they were brave enough to feed the class pet. Brielle-Elaine was so excited. She answered and asked questions right along with them. She couldn't wait to tell her mom that she was right. Being herself was all she needed to be.

Printed in the United States
by Baker & Taylor Publisher Services